I'm Tired of Lions

I'm Tired of Lions

WRITTEN AND ILLUSTRATED BY

Zhenya Gay

THE VIKING PRESS · NEW YORK

Little Leo sat and looked at his breakfast. Just sat and looked.

"What is wrong, dear?" asked Little Leo's mother, Mrs. Lion.

"I'm not hungry, Mother," said Little Leo.

6

"Are you sick?" asked Mrs. Lion. She worried about Little Leo. He was her only cub.

"No, Mother, I'm not sick. I'm tired of lions," said Little Leo.

"But, dear, you ARE a lion," said Mrs. Lion. "You have fine claws. Soon you'll be old enough to have a fine roar."

"I'm tired of lions. I'm tired of claws. I don't ever want to roar," said Little Leo. "I wish I wasn't a lion."

"Well, dear, we can't change that," said Mrs. Lion. "Come, eat your breakfast."

But Little Leo just pushed at his food. Then he looked at his mother and cried, "I can change that!" He sounded happy for the first time that morning.

"Dear, you can't change that. Do eat your breakfast," coaxed Mrs. Lion.

Little Leo ate one mouthful. He looked at his mother again. "Mother," he said, "I know HOW I can change."

"Indeed? Would you like to tell Mother?" asked Mrs. Lion.

"I can be someone else!" said Little Leo.

8

"Oho!" said Mrs. Lion. "Who else can you be, dear?"
"I can be

9

a giraffe," said Little Leo.

"Is your neck long enough to reach to the tops of tall trees?" asked Mrs. Lion.

"No," answered Little Leo, "but I can be a

monkey!"
12

"Can you climb trees and hang from a branch by one paw?" asked Mrs. Lion.

"No," said Little Leo, "but a

bird, Mother, I can be a bird!"

"Dear Little Leo," said Mrs. Lion, "birds can fly. No lion can fly. How can you be a bird?"

"Well, I suppose I can't be a bird," agreed Little Leo. He thought for a moment.

14

"A toad," he said, "I can be a toad!"

"Can you take off your coat, Little Leo?" asked Mrs. Lion.

"No," said Little Leo. He thought and thought.

"I know," he said, "I can be

a hippopotamus!"

"Can you swim in lakes and rivers and walk under water?" asked Mrs. Lion.

"No. I don't even like to swim," said Little Leo sadly. He thought some more. "But an

17

elephant. I know I can be an elephant. Can't I?"

"Is your nose long enough and strong enough to carry
things?" asked Mrs. Lion.

"No, Mother," answered Little Leo. "Oh, dear, what
CAN I be?"

"I think you can be

a fine lion when you grow up," said Mrs. Lion.

"But, Mother, I'm tired of lions. I'm tired of claws. I'm tired of roars. I wish I wasn't a lion," said Little Leo.

"I know, dear," said Mrs. Lion, "but one of these days you'll be happy to be a lion."

Little Leo didn't hear what his mother had said. He was thinking again. "Mother," he cried, "I've thought of someone else. A big snake. That's what I can be!"

"A big snake has no legs. You have four legs, dear," explained Mrs. Lion. "And a big snake can squeeze," she added.

"Oh!" shouted Little Leo happily. "I CAN be a big snake. I can squeeze. See?" he said and squeezed his mother hard. "I love you, Mother. Even though you are a lion."

"Dear little lion cub," said Mrs. Lion, "I love you too."

"My, MY, what's this?" asked Little Leo's father, Mr. Lion, as he came to breakfast.

"I'm a big snake, Father. I can squeeze," cried Little Leo. "See, Father?" he said and squeezed his father hard.

"Well, I must say you can squeeze, son," said Mr. Lion. "But I must also say that you don't look like a big snake to me. What big snake ever had four legs like yours?" he added as he began to eat his breakfast.

Little Leo looked at his four legs. I guess I can't be a big snake, he thought. He began to cry.

"My, MY, what's this?" exclaimed Mr. Lion.

"Now, Father, we were just pretending," said Mrs. Lion. "At the moment our son doesn't want to be a lion. He wants to change into someone else."

"What's wrong with being what you are, son?" asked Mr. Lion.

"I'm tired of lions. I'm tired of claws. I'm tired of roars. I wish I wasn't a lion," answered Little Leo tearfully.

"Well," said Mr. Lion, "I don't know what children are coming to these days. Excuse me, Mother," he said to Mrs. Lion. "I'm going to take a nap. Breakfast and all this changing about have made me sleepy."

"Have a nice nap, Father," said Mrs. Lion. "Now, Little Leo, dry your tears. Eat your breakfast or you won't grow strong enough to be anyone at all."

"I'm not hungry," said Little Leo, trying not to cry.

"Come, now. I have an idea," said Mrs. Lion. "You've let your breakfast get cold. Why don't you take it with you and go where the grass is short? It rained during the night, but the sun is shining now. It's a beautiful day and will cheer you," she said in a coaxing voice.

"Do I have to go?" asked Little Leo.

"Try it, dear. I'm sure you'll feel happier if you do. Eat your breakfast. After that perhaps we can pretend some more," said Mrs. Lion.

"You mean you'll help?" cried Little Leo.

"Of course, dear," said Mrs. Lion.

Little Leo picked up his cold breakfast and went where the grass was short. It was a beautiful sunny day. He watched blue and red and orange butterflies. Little Leo ate a mouthful of breakfast. He saw blue and red and orange flowers. It was a beautiful day. Little Leo ate another mouthful of breakfast. And then another. And another and another until he'd eaten all of his breakfast. He did feel happier, just as his mother had said he would.

"I think I'll take a walk. Perhaps I can find someone I've never seen before. Then I could surprise Mother," he said to himself.

Little Leo hadn't walked very far before he came to a

24

puddle left by last night's rain. It was as bright and clear as a mirror. Little Leo had never seen a bright, clear puddle of rain before. He stood just above it. He wasn't very much above it, for he was only a small lion cub. Little Leo looked into the puddle.

He blinked his two bright eyes. He looked again. He couldn't believe what he saw.

"Oh, oh, OH!" he cried. "You're the nicest animal I've ever seen! I'd rather be you than anyone else." Little Leo

turned and ran back to his mother calling, "Mother! MOTHER! Come and look!"

"My goodness, dear, what is wrong?" asked Mrs. Lion.

"Nothing is wrong, Mother," said Little Leo, "please, Mother. Come and look. Hurry, HURRY!" he shouted.

"Gracious me!" exclaimed Mrs. Lion. "Just a moment. And don't make so much noise, dear. You'll wake your father, and that would never do."

"But, Mother," begged Little Leo, "you promised you'd help. And I've found the nicest animal I've ever seen. I'd rather be him than anyone else. Please hurry," he said as softly as he could.

Mrs. Lion, of course, kept her promise. She followed Little Leo to the rain puddle. But then Little Leo thought, suppose that nice animal isn't in the puddle? Suppose he ran away? Oh dear. Little Leo took a deep breath and looked into the puddle.

"Mother, look, LOOK!" he cried.

Mrs. Lion looked. Mrs. Lion smiled. She took Little Leo into her paws and squeezed him hard, quite like a big snake. "Little Leo," she asked, "don't you know who that is?"

Little Leo looked at his mother in surprise. "No," he said. 'But, Mother, do YOU know? Who is it? Can I be it?"

"Dear Little Leo, you ARE it," said Mrs. Lion.

"I am?" asked Little Leo. "But how can I be it? I'm here."

"That's true, dear. But look into the puddle again.

27

"With me this time," said Mrs. Lion.

Little Leo looked into the puddle again. Right beside him he saw his mother's beautiful face. He didn't understand.

28

He looked up at his mother.

Mrs. Lion licked Little Leo's face gently with her rough tongue. Then she explained, "That is your reflection, dear. When water is still and clear and smooth, you can see yourself in it."

"Oh," said Little Leo.

"Is that all you have to say?" asked Mrs. Lion. "I thought I heard you say you'd rather be your new animal than anyone else."

"I did," agreed Little Leo, "but that was before I knew it was a lion. I'm tired of lions and I'm tired —"

"Now, dear," said Mrs. Lion, "listen to me. When you first looked into the puddle you were happy and pleased with what you saw. And what you saw was you."

"I guess I was," said Little Leo.

"Well, dear. After all, you are a lion. And I told you no-body could change that. Come, look into the puddle again," coaxed Mrs. Lion.

Little Leo did. "Is that really a lion?" he asked.

"Not yet, dear. I am a lion. Your father is a lion. But you will be a lion soon," explained Mrs. Lion.

Little Leo looked at his reflection. He twitched his small whiskers. So did his reflection. "Look at me, Mother. I think I do like what I see."

"Good," said Mrs. Lion.

"I never have roared," said Little Leo.

"I wonder if I could."

"Try it," said Mrs. Lion.

"Wr-r-rrrr," said Little Leo.

"Good," said Mrs. Lion. "You will be a fine lion when you grow up."

Little Leo spent quite a long time looking into the puddle and practicing roars. He turned to his mother and asked:

30

"Mother, I CAN be a lion, can't I?"

"Yes, dear, you can," said Mrs. Lion.

And now the happiest lion cub in the whole world is Little Leo.

He was so thrilled to have finally jumped it that he looked back to admire once again his silvery wings, but to his astonishment they were gone!

GREAT SCOTT—he had jumped the brook without the wings!

AND CLEARED THE BROOK, WITH

PLENTY OF ROOM TO SPARE.

So he backed up to get a good running start—

And there, right in front of him, was the same brook that he had tried so many times to jump. It would be easy now with his silver wings!

As he moved, he woke up.

But it didn't leave him alone and Flip snapped
at it.

Flip was enjoying all this very much but he did wish that a big horsefly droning and buzzing around him would leave him alone.

Swish, the cat, jumped on the back of Willy-the-Goat to get a better view.

Old Scratch-and-Cackle, seeing on the ground the shadow of a flying horse, thought the world was coming to an end. She fled to the nearest sunflower and gathered her chicks beneath her. But not one of them could keep his eyes from the skies.

Piggly-Woof saw him coming and was so scared that his tail uncurled, stood up straight, and stayed that way.

This was the greatest fun he had ever imagined. He wanted only one thing more—that his friends on the farm should see him jumping higher and further than any horse had ever jumped before. So he swooped down over the barn.

A little more effort and he was saying "Hello" to the iron horse that told which way the wind was blowing. Flip was sorry for him. "He can only run in a circle," he thought; "I can fly anywhere!"

It was such a success that he didn't want to stop a minute. On he went over the split rail fences.

He thought: "With these wings I can jump over anything I please! That haystack should be easy."

He was so excited that his knees knocked. His hair stood on end.

Suddenly he felt his shoulders itching. He looked around. He had grown a pair of beautiful silvery wings.

As he slept, he dreamed.

One day he tried so hard and so long that he tired himself out and fell asleep wishing—wishing that he could jump the brook like his mother —perhaps higher and further!

When he did jump, he always landed in the water instead of on the opposite bank.

Other times he wouldn't stop soon enough and would fall in.

He tried and tried. Sometimes he would run right up to the edge and stop suddenly.

To get away from these antics, his mother would often jump over the brook to graze. Flip would be left whinnying on the other side. "Oh, if I could only jump as she does!" he would sigh.

He could do plenty of other things. He could kick and buck and fairly twist himself inside out, or run circles around his mother, sometimes nipping her and pulling her tail.

Every day that they came to the stream Flip's mother would jump lightly over it and back again. Flip thought this a beautiful sight and wished that he could do it.

It wasn't long before his mother was teaching him to walk and then to run. Flip thought this was great fun.

His home was a large farm in Kentucky with miles and miles of split rail fences and big trees. A clear, sparkling stream wound in and out among the green fields. Flip wanted to get out there and play.

Flip was born.

To Linda and Karen

FIRST PUBLISHED MARCH 1941
THIRTEENTH PRINTING MARCH 1966
PIC BK

FLIP

STORY AND PICTURES BY WESLEY DENNIS

NEW YORK · THE VIKING PRESS

FLIP